NICK JR.
DORA the EXPLORER®

Dora's Starry Christmas

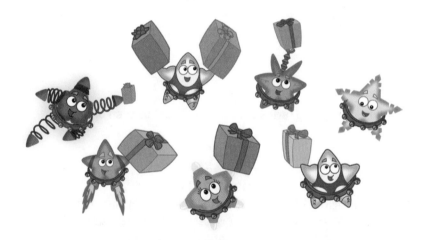

by Christine Ricci
illustrated by A&J Studios

Simon Spotlight/Nick Jr.

New York   London   Toronto   Sydney

Based on the TV series *Dora the Explorer*® as seen on Nick Jr.®

SIMON SPOTLIGHT
An imprint of Simon & Schuster Children's Publishing Division
1230 Avenue of the Americas, New York, New York 10020
© 2005 Viacom International Inc. All rights reserved.
Nick JR., *Dora the Explorer*, and all related titles, logos, and characters are registered
trademarks of Viacom International Inc.
All rights reserved, including the right of reproduction in whole or in part in any form.
SIMON SPOTLIGHT and colophon are registered trademarks of Simon & Schuster, Inc.
Manufactured in the United States of America
6 8 10 9 7 5
ISBN-13: 978-1-4169-0249-2
ISBN-10: 1-4169-0249-X
0909 LAK

It was Christmas Eve, and everyone at Dora's house was getting excited for the celebration. Dora's baby brother and sister couldn't wait for Dora to tell them the story of Santa and his reindeer.

"Far, far away in a little toy shop at the North Pole lives a jolly old man called Santa Claus," began Dora.

"Oooohh!" cooed the babies.
Dora continued, "Every Christmas Eve, Santa's flying reindeer pull his sleigh around the world, so he can deliver presents."

Just then they heard a *whoosh* and a *swoosh* right outside the door!

"I wonder who that could be," said Dora.

Everyone ran outside just in time to see Santa's sleigh and his eight flying reindeer land in the front yard!

"*¡Ayúdenme, por favor!* I need your help," called Santa.

"Achoooooo!" sneezed the reindeer.

Santa explained that his reindeer had gotten colds.
"If my reindeer aren't feeling their best, then I can't fly around the world delivering presents. My Christmas surprises will be ruined!" cried Santa.

"I can help the reindeer get well," said Diego. He wrapped each reindeer in a cozy, warm blanket and made some special carrot soup for them to eat.

"Now they just need some time to rest and they'll be all better!" Diego said.

"But how will my sleigh fly without my reindeer?" wondered Santa.

Dora knew that Santa would need help to make all of his Christmas deliveries. Suddenly she had an idea.

"The Explorer Stars can fly your sleigh and help you save Christmas!" she exclaimed.

"Explorer Stars, come quick!" called Dora. "We need your help!"

Eight Explorer Stars flew out of Dora's glowing star pocket and hitched themselves to Santa's sleigh.

"I'll stay here and care for the reindeer," said Diego as *Mami, Papi, Abuela,* and the babies waved good-bye.

"Up, up, and away we go!" called Santa as Supra, Ultra, and Mega Stars used their strength to pull the sleigh high into the night sky.

With Rocket Star's help the sleigh flew faster than ever before. Soon it arrived at the first stop. Santa asked Dora and Boots to help him deliver all the presents to the whales, fish, and turtles in the ocean.

"Merry Christmas, everyone!" called Boots as he and Dora carefully launched each present.

Next the Explorer Stars flew the sleigh to the tallest mountain. Saltador helped the sleigh superjump all the way to the top, so Santa and his helpers could give gifts to all of the sleeping mountain animals.

Then Saltador did a super-duper jump to deliver a present to the Moon while Helada Star turned the trees into a beautiful winter wonderland.

Throughout the night the Explorer Stars pulled the sleigh to all the small towns and big cities. The sleigh landed on every rooftop so that Santa and his helpers could fill each stocking and deliver presents to every girl, boy, and animal.

They were careful not to miss anyone . . . not even the littlest mouse.

On the way to deliver presents in the Rainforest, clouds covered up the Moon.

"I can't see," said Santa. "I need more light."

"Don't worry," said Dora. "Glowy Star can help!"

So Glowy shined her lights extra bright.

"Now do you see the Rainforest?" asked Dora.
"I see it!" called Santa as he steered the sleigh toward the treetops.

Next the Explorer Stars flew the sleigh toward a barn,
a garden, and a tree house.

"Can you find presents for Benny, Isa, and Tico?" asked
Santa. Dora and Boots searched through the sleigh until they
found some special presents for their friends.

"And here's a present for Swiper!" exclaimed Dora. "I guess Swiper really likes Christmas," giggled Boots when he spotted Swiper's foxhole.

Finally, at sunrise, Santa guided the sleigh back to Dora's house. To Santa's joy his reindeer were feeling much better!

"Thank you for helping my reindeer and for delivering the Christmas presents. I couldn't have done it without all of you," said Santa. He reached into his nearly empty sack and pulled out an extra-special present for his helpers.

When they unwrapped the present they found a special music box.

"This music box will always remind you of the night you helped save Christmas," said Santa.

"*¡Gracias!*" exclaimed Dora, Boots, and Diego.

"Now let's celebrate!" cheered Santa.

"We did it!" cheered Dora. "*¡Feliz Navidad!* Merry Christmas!"